COUNTING
SHEEP

Written by Pippa Chorley   Illustrated by Danny Deeptown

 Marshall Cavendish
Children

For my very own flock, James, Lochie, Calum and Caitlin

~ P.C

For Eleri, River, and Ewan the sheep, who helps us all get some sleep

~ D.D

One dark stormy night, when Sam couldn't sleep,
Her mum suggested, "Try counting some sheep."

Sam closed her eyes and pictured a flock,
But the white, woolly sheep were running...AMOK!

They all baa-ed and bleated, then one sheep made sense.
"Little Shep," he said, "can't jump over the fence."

"He's too small, you see, and the fence is too high.
But I've had an idea, we can see if he'll fly!"

They huddled together and built him some wings,
Out of feathers and sticks, paper,
glue and string.

But as hard as he tried to fly through the air,
His hooves wouldn't move and Shep went nowhere.

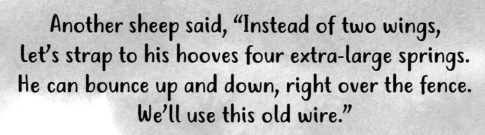

Another sheep said, "Instead of two wings,
let's strap to his hooves four extra-large springs.
He can bounce up and down, right over the fence.
We'll use this old wire."

Shep gulped and looked tense.

The first bounce was bonkers,
Shep whooshed through the crowd.

The next bounce went higher,
He whizzed through a cloud!

But it wouldn't have mattered if Shep had reached space,
For he always came back to the very same place.

"What about a ramp?" one shouted with glee.
"We'll use bales of hay, it will work, you'll see."

Shep looked nervous as they stacked them up high,

His legs turned to jelly as the bales reached the sky.

When Shep tried to climb,
his legs were a muddle,

They wibbled and wobbled till he fell in a puddle.

"Let's make him a slingshot," said a fat, fluffy pair.
But a small voice said, "No!"

The sheep stopped and stared.

They all turned to Sam, who pushed through the flock.
"I want no more contraptions!"

The sheep baa-ed in shock.

"Then what will we do, for you cannot sleep?
And we can't do our job, if we're not jumping sheep."

"Let's make the fence lower. He can jump just like you,
And as Shep grows taller, so can the fence too."

"You can measure him first, using this string.
It's got to be simpler than ramps, springs and wings!"

The flock all agreed and thought Sam very wise.
They began to rebuild the fence the right size.

Shep held his breath
and took a great leap...

And as Shep cleared the fence,
Sam at last fell asleep.

© 2019 Pippa Chorley
Illustrations © Danny Deeptown

Published by Marshall Cavendish Children
An imprint of Marshall Cavendish International

All rights reserved

Other Marshall Cavendish Offices:
Marshall Cavendish Corporation. 99 White Plains Road, Tarrytown NY 10591-9001, USA • Marshall Cavendish
International (Thailand) Co Ltd. 253 Asoke, 12th Flr, Sukhumvit 21 Road, Klongtoey Nua, Wattana, Bangkok 10110,
Thailand • Marshall Cavendish (Malaysia) Sdn Bhd, Times Subang, Lot 46, Subang Hi-Tech Industrial Park,
Batu Tiga, 40000 Shah Alam, Selangor Darul Ehsan, Malaysia.

Marshall Cavendish is a registered trademark of Times Publishing Limited

National Library Board, Singapore Cataloguing-in-Publication Data

Name(s): Chorley, Pippa. | Deeptown, Danny, illustrator.
Title: Counting sheep / written by Pippa Chorley ; illustrated by Danny Deeptown.
Description: Singapore : Marshall Cavendish, [2019]
Identifier(s): OCN 1088514646 | ISBN 978-981-48-4119-1 (hardcover)
Subject(s): LCSH: Bedtime--Juvenile fiction. | Counting--Juvenile fiction. | Sleep--Juvenile fiction.
Classification: DDC 428.6--dc23

Printed in Malaysia